THE LAST BADGE

GEORGE McClements

HYPERION BOOKS FOR CHILDREN
New York

Dedication Badge

4

Rachel, Sammy & Matthew

Information Badge

For information address Hyperion Books for Children,
114 Fifth Avenue, New York, New York 10011-5690.
Printed in Singapore
First Edition
1 3 5 7 9 10 8 6 4 2
Library of Congress Cataloging-in-Publication Data on file.
ISBN 0-7868-0956-6
Reinforced binding
Visit www.hyperionbooksforchildren.com

This year a young Grizzly Scout named Samuel Moss was determined to earn a place in his family's Album of Scouting Greatness.

For twelve generations, the Album of Scouting Greatness had been part of the Moss family. Samuel knew that within its pages were mementos of great Grizzly Scout achievements performed by uncles, grandfathers, cousins, a dog (that's a long story), and even Samuel's father (he had earned a Golden Salmon Award!).

Although Samuel often dreamed about looking through
the album, there was a rule that made it impossible.

*RULE:

YOU HAVE TO BE <u>IN</u> THE ALBUM TO LOOK AT THE ALBUM. . . . SORRY.

Samuel hadn't performed a great feat...yet.

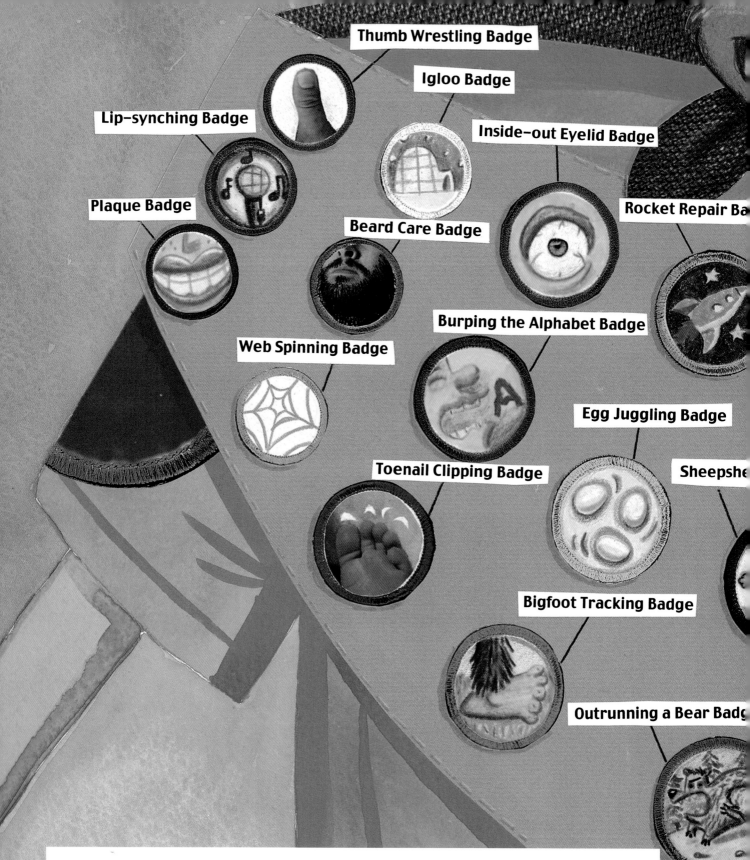

Thumb Wrestling Badge

Igloo Badge

Lip-synching Badge

Inside-out Eyelid Badge

Plaque Badge

Rocket Repair Ba

Beard Care Badge

Burping the Alphabet Badge

Web Spinning Badge

Egg Juggling Badge

Toenail Clipping Badge

Sheepshe

Bigfoot Tracking Badge

Outrunning a Bear Badg

He was no slouch, mind you. Within a short time Samuel had earned every badge the Grizzly Scouts had to offer.

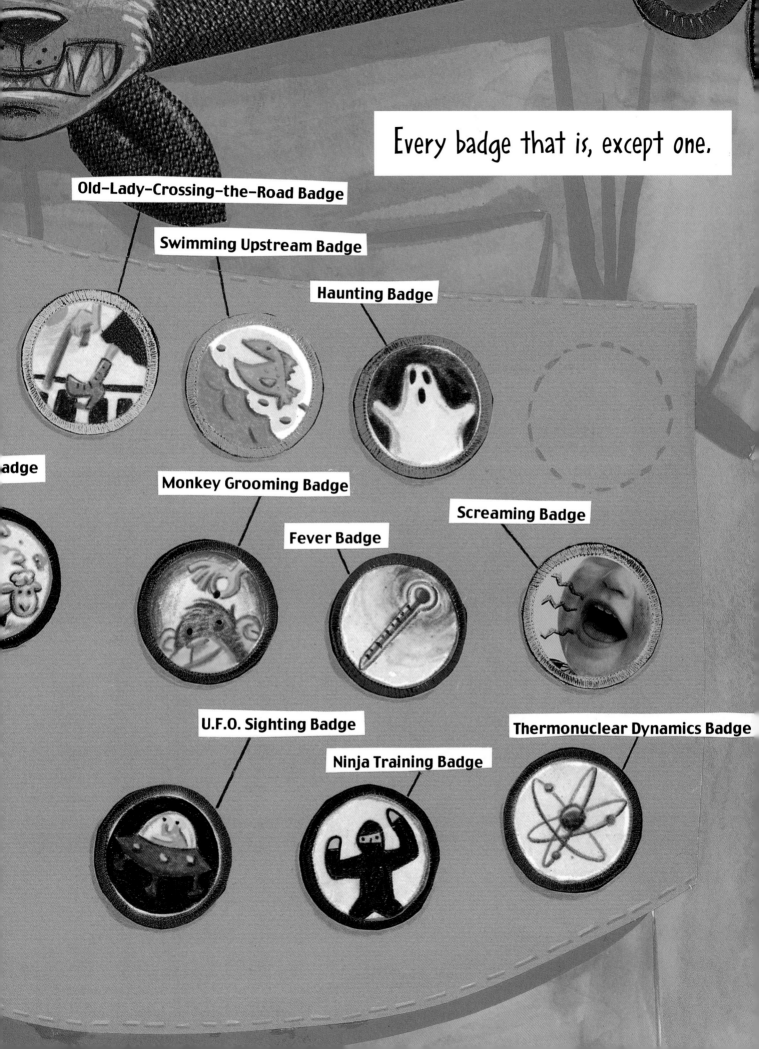

Every badge that is, except one.

Old-Lady-Crossing-the-Road Badge

Swimming Upstream Badge

Haunting Badge

...adge

Monkey Grooming Badge

Screaming Badge

Fever Badge

U.F.O. Sighting Badge

Thermonuclear Dynamics Badge

Ninja Training Badge

The ever elusive Moon Frog Badge. In fact, no scout had ever earned the badge...

The MOON FROG BADGE

What are you doing looking down here? There is really nothing to see, honestly. You should be reading the next page. It has a lot of interesting information.

o earn the badge, a scout must provide evidence of the Moon Frog.

According to myth, the Moon Frog hibernates for years at a time. It awakens when a solitary moonbeam shines upon its resting place.

This occurs only once every 30 years at the 12th hour of the 10th night of the 8th month. The lack of data makes calculating the exact location of the Moon Frog a nearly impossible task.

possibly due to the incredibly difficult task of finding a Moon Frog.

This was it—his chance for greatness. Samuel would become the first Grizzly Scout to earn the MOON FROG BADGE!

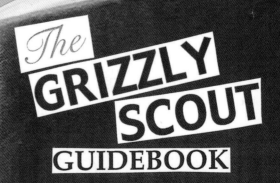

Aha!

Days flew by as Samuel hunted through exotic bookstores and libraries, searching for anything written about the Moon Frog.

Saturn

Mars

Earth

Moon

Pluto

Weeks turned into months as he studied planets and stars. He measured alignment angles and calculated moonbeam refractions. Entire weekends were spent photographing frogs of all shapes and sizes, just to be ready.

"Say Ribbit"

Then, one fateful night, after all the long hours…

Hey, come back!

and countless failures…

SUCCESS!

He had found the location of the Moon Frog.

Samuel shared his exciting news with his father, who pointed out a major problem!

Samuel had been so focused on locating the Moon Frog that he had failed to notice that the 12th hour of the 10th night of the 8th month was that very night!

He had only... **3 HOURS!!**

With no time to spare, the duo packed everything they would need for an overnight excursion and headed for the car.

The trek to the Moon Frog was a long, perilous journey. Samuel's directions had to be followed precisely, or the two would risk becoming lost forever.

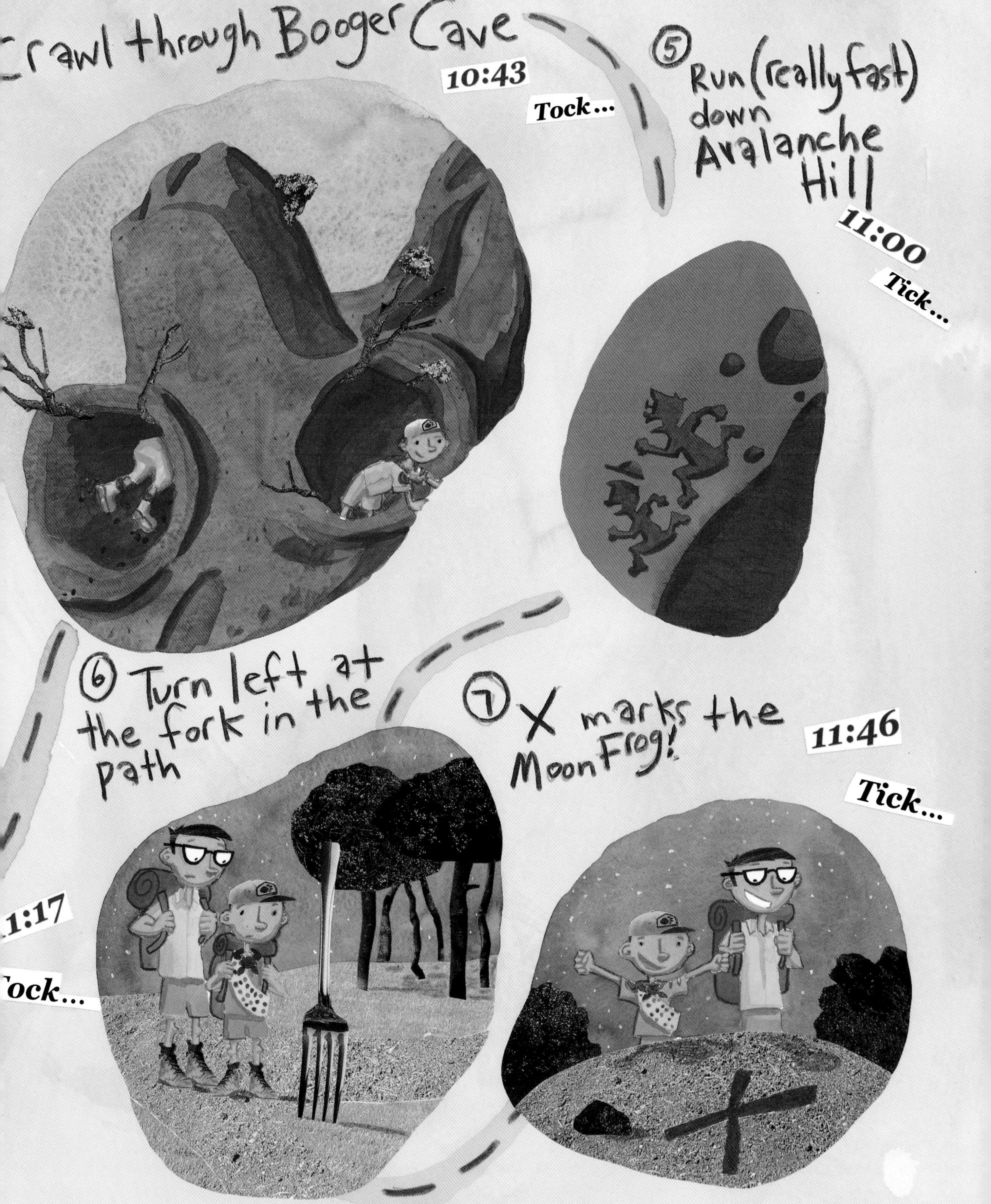

They finally arrived at the campsite.

11:46! Samuel only had <u>14</u> minutes until a moonbeam would awaken the sleeping Moon Frog! He had to act quickly.

11:50

Apply frog camouflage.

11:54

Grab camera. (Oh, no! Too many practice shots. Only one photo left.)

11:57
Run to the
Moon Frog site.

11:59

Stretch
photo finger
(can't afford
to cramp).

12:00

. . . showtime!

Soon a stirring caused
a few bubbles to surface....

Then two eyes popped from the mud and blinked....

blink... blink...

Next, a head emerged,
followed by a long
leg with
wiggling
toes....

Finally, an entire Moon Frog appeared and, much to Samuel's
surprise, unfurled a magnificent crest!

Samuel paused for a moment to admire the amazing frog.
Then he sprang back into action and snapped a photo.

HE DID IT! HE DID IT! HE DID IT!

Samuel Moss had become the first Grizzly Scout ever to capture a photo of the Moon Frog!

He would be famous.

His photo would appear on the cover of *Grizzly Scout Weekly*.

The mayor would present him with the Moon Frog Badge.

He would, of course, get his own talk show, and most important, he would earn his place in the Album of Scouting Greatness!

When the news spread of his accomplishment, scientists from around the world would flock to meet him.

He would show them his calculations and where he had found the Moon Frog.

They would admire him for being so clever.

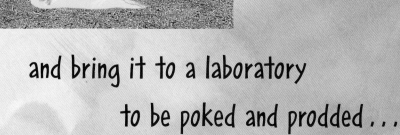

But what if they wanted
to study the Moon Frog?
They would dig it up...

and bring it to a laboratory
        to be poked and prodded...

only to spend the rest of
its life in a glass jar!

Moonicus Frogium

Samuel couldn't let that happen to such an incredible animal. He would keep the Moon Frog's photo and location a secret.

Back at the camp, Samuel told his father the whole story. The family tradition of great scouts would not continue with him.

His father looked shocked.

Then he handed Samuel the Album of Scouting Greatness.

To Samuel's surprise, the album wasn't packed with heroic scouting feats. Instead, it was filled with pages and pages of . . .

Moon Frogs!

1880

1910

1940

1970

1970

Samuel's father explained that every generation of the Moss family had found the Moon Frog and, just like Samuel, they had decided to keep its location a secret.

the
ALBUM
of

By protecting the Moon Frog, Samuel had become part
of his family's tradition.

Finally, he was a great Grizzly Scout.

That night, Samuel's father regaled him with tales of past Moon Frog outings. They fell asleep while trading photography tips.

...Ribbit...Ribbit...Ribbit...
...Ribbit...Ribbit...Ribbit...
...Ribbi...